Auschwitz: A Love Story

By Curtis R. Crim

ISBN: 978-0-9888255-0-5

Printed in the United States of America

First Printing

This story is dedicated to my family, without whom, I might actually be sane.

TABLE OF CONTENTS

Introduction: The Concept

Be warned; this book might be the most horrifying, disgusting, nauseating, and nasty book ever written.

This was not the goal.

Originally, the concept started out as a comic bit on positive spin. My idea was to think of the most horrible things that humans have ever experienced (and done to each other), and put a positive spin on them.

For instance, a woman gives birth to a still born child, but she is glad, because she *hates* kids.

Or… The police come to the door and tell a man that his wife has died in a car accident. He's like, "Awesome! I *hated* that bitch!

Another example: A man is sentenced by the king to be tortured daily for a year before being executed, but it is okay, because he is a masochist, loves being tortured, and hated his wife anyway. He and the torturer look forward to their daily sessions, because each one is doing what he really loves the most in life!

This story is based on one of the concepts that came up related to the "Positive Spin" comedic bit.

However, as it took shape, I saw the opportunity to create a vision of the world that might be more twisted and simply wrong that anything anyone else had ever portrayed. I personally also find it amazingly humorous, but even if you don't find yourself laughing, it will still almost certainly freak you out totally, which has become part of the goal.

Note: Given the geographical location and timeline of this story, assume that most of the dialog is in Yiddish, Polish, or German.

After careful consideration, I have decided that some scenes in this story can be interpreted as being a little anti-Semitic. This being said, I want to say that I am part Jewish on my mother's side. As a Jew, I have the right to hate myself and my people as much as I want without being accused of being an anti-Semitist.

This book contains adult situations, and **is** appropriate for readers off all ages.

This kind of humor is not for everyone, but it you give it a chance, you might find it really really funny!

I sincerely hope that even the most demented and twisted reader will still find himself shocked and disturbed by what he reads in this book.

If you are *not* disturbed by the events in this story, then do everyone a favor and SEE A FUCKING PSYCHIATRIST!

Chapter One: Youth

Lechoslaw

Poland - 1929

Crack! Whack! "Aaah! Aaah!"

The black leather whip came down repeatedly on the naked back of the bloody and trembling boy.

"You little bastard!" his mother yelled, and whipped him even harder, throwing her weight into this time. Her words were slurred, and she struggled to maintain balance.

"No Mother! I didn't do anything wrong!" pleaded the small boy.

Whack! Again, even harder this time. "It doesn't matter!" she yelled back.

He hated it when she got this drunk, because she wouldn't even remember doing it.

As the whip came down, Lechoslaw let the pain wash over him, and let his mind drift back to when he was younger. He used to try to hide her whip, but she would always find it and then punish him for hiding it.

Now, almost ten years old, he has come to feel that the beatings were just the way his mother expressed love. He used to think that he just deserved to be abused, but now a feeling of excitement comes to him whenever he feels her inflicting pain on him. "I wonder whether this is normal." he thought to himself.

Bozydar

The closet door flew open and a small girl ran out yelling.

"Daddy! Daddy! Bozydar is trying to hurt me again!" she shouted.

A tall dark haired man ran into the room and picked the girl up. "Darling, are you okay? How's Daddy's baby girl?"

He put the girl down, who then rushed out of the room. The man dragged the boy from the closet and yelled.

"What were you trying to do to your little sister boy? Didn't I teach you enough of a lesson last time?"

Bozydar despised his father. His punishments were *way* overboard and usually for the most minor of violations of his rules. His mother was terrified of her husband, and would do nothing in his defense.

Bozydar let himself get carried away by his hatred for his father, and over time came to enjoy tormenting and then later torturing small creatures.

Celestynka, on the other hand, he loved. He had always loved and worshiped her, but he also enjoyed wrestling around with her and touching her in inappropriate places. He enjoyed caressing her thighs and buttocks. He always felt a pulsing in his loins whenever she was around. He loved to kiss her on the lips, but she would always push him away and complain to their father whenever he tried to use his tongue.

"I can't help it. I would never do anything to hurt Celestynka; I love her! Please don't hit me, father!" Bozydar pleaded to no avail.

"You brought this on yourself boy!" the main exclaimed.

The man held the boy's arm with an iron tight grip with his left hand, and reached into the closet. His right hand emerged with a large heavy duty open end wrench.

Bozydar held his hands over his head in a vain attempt to defend himself. As he screamed, the wrench came down on his right arm, and he could hear it crack. He cradled it with his left arm as pain shot through his body. Again, the wrench was lifted into the air, this time coming down on the side of his head.

Bozydar could hear his own voice screaming as everything went black.

Dog

When Bozydar awoke the next morning, his head throbbed and he discovered that he was covered in fresh bruises. Apparently, his dad had continued to beat him for quite some time after he had lost consciousness. When his father got that mad, he would also black out and not be entirely in control of what he was doing, or even remember it clearly.

On the way to school, Bozydar did not want to be seen by the other students, because he was embarrassed and didn't want to have to explain his black eye.

He decided to take a shortcut through the woods of which he knew. That way he could get to school early and pick a fight with the school bully. He would get his ass kicked, but would have an explanation for his injuries, and not have to tell anyone that his father had beaten him.

The path in the woods took Bozydar past a dense stand of evergreens. He noticed something lying at the edge of the grove. As he got closer, he could see that it was a dead dog. "Yea, you're the lucky one." he said aloud, and noticed tire marks on it. It must have been hit in the road, and crawled out here to die.

He crossed the bridge over a small creek and was soon at school. He didn't have to provoke the school bully, who apparently had already planed to kick his ass that morning.

Throughout the school day, he found his mind strangely drifting back to the dead dog he had seen in the woods, and decided to go home on the same path.

Bozydar hated school. He hated his teachers, who always seemed to have it in for him. He hated the other students because they were cruel and humiliated him. He hated the curriculum, and the classes seemed meaningless and boring to him.

When school *finally* let out for the day, Bozydar ran out of the school and to the woods.

When he arrived back at the stand of evergreens, he saw that the dog was still there.

He looked around and made sure that he was alone. "Fuck you Dad! I fucking hate you!" He shouted, and kicked the dog in the ribs. It felt really good, so he repeated the action, this time kicking it in the face, and added, "I am going to fucking kill you, you old bastard!"

He felt an exhilaration come over him, and for a reason he was not entirely sure of, he stuck his right index finger into the dog's anus, which he found to still be pliable. The dog must have expired just that day.

The corpse's anal orifice was very tight though, so he licked the index and middle fingers of his right hand and again forced them up into the dog's ass. He then used his fingers to stretch the rectum as wide as he could.

With his left hand, he removed his penis from his pants and smeared saliva on it before shoving his cock into the dog's asshole.

"Fuck you! Fuck you! Fuck you!" he yelled, and he came fucking the dead corpse.

Bozydar emitted a large exhale and leaned over to the dog's face and gave it a kiss. "You're mine now honey." he said to the dog, and then pulled his cock out of its ass, and then sniffed his fingers.

He slipped his dick back into pants and picked up the dog, and turned around heading back in the direction of the school.

When he got to the creek, he went down and waded along the creek bed until he found the perfect spot in which to hide the dog. He placed the dog in an outcropping where it would be less likely to be seen, and positioned it so that the posterior of the dog would be in the water. That way, it will remain soft and easy to enter. He then covered the anterior of the dog with leaves, so that it would not be seen.

On the way home, he decided to take the short cut through the woods every day until the dog had deteriorated to the point where it could not be used anymore.

Fag

"Fucking faggot!" "Yea!" "Get him!" The kids all shouted at Lechoslaw.

Lechoslaw tried to run, but there were too many of them, and they had surrounded him.

"They said you got a boner in the gym locker room!" someone shouted.

It's true. Lechoslaw always knew that he liked boys. He was always getting crushes on boys at school, but had not had a problem getting uncontrollable erections in the past. He knew that this was taboo, and that he would be shunned by the other kids who attended his school.

One of his attackers shoved him to the ground, and the mob moved in, hitting and kicking him. There were so many fists and feet coming at him that he could not struggle back to his feet. He decided to just try to cover his face and curl up in a protected posture.

Eventually, the attacking children ran out of steam, and as the mob dissipated, one of the larger boys spit in his face and called him a faggot one final time before walking off.

Birthday

Lechoslaw dragged himself home, beaten and bruised, with his clothing torn and dirty. He had a black eye, a bloody nose, a bloody lip, and various smaller scrapes, cuts, and abrasions.

He walked in hoping that his mother would offer some sympathy.

"What in the Hell happened to you?" she demanded, leaning on the wall with one hand and holding a drink in the other.

"I was beaten up on the way home from school again!" he said, his voice wavering, as though about to cry.

"Well, it's your birthday today, and I was planning to do something special with you, but *NO*, as usual, *you've* managed to disappoint me! You tore your clothing which *I* have to pay for and you are bleeding in *my* house. You know where all the bleeding is done here!" she yelled.

"No, Mom, please!" he pleaded, but it seemed to have no impact.

She grabbed the boy and dragged him screaming over to the basement door. Flinging open the door, she picked up the child and threw him down the stairs. His head hit a post on the way down, and it was *lights out* for Lechoslaw.

When he opened his eyes, he was lying on a couch in the basement, and his mother was standing over him, whip in hand… and far drunker than before.

"You have been a very naughty little girl, haven't you?" she said, words slurred.

"Mommy?" He looked down and saw that she had dressed him up in some of her clothes, including a skirt and a bra that was stuffed with tissue paper.

"You have been a bad little girl and gotten into my makeup again, haven't you?" she persisted. "Go ahead, look."

He turned to a mirror on the wall of the basement. She had put one of her wigs and some makeup on him too, and he had to admit that he did look a little like a girl.

"Bad little girls have to be punished. Tell me that you know that you have been bad and that you *need* to be punished." she demanded.

Lechoslaw knew that there was no point in resisting her, and he had grown to look forward to her punishments. Besides, he had forgotten it was his birthday, with all the beatings, and perhaps she will go easy on him today. "You are right." he said, "I have been a *bad* little girl and I *need* to be punished!"

"Then *ask* to be punished. Beg me for it!" she said sharply.

He fell to his knees and said, "Yes, Mommy, please punish me, I beg you!"

She produced some sash cord and tied his hands together, then tied them to a supporting post in the middle of the basement. She then lifted his skirt to expose his ass.

"You are wearing a pair of *my* panties! For this, you must get a spanking!" she said, her breath getting faster.

She slapped him on the ass as hard as she could until she felt weak and her hands were sore. His ass was red from the punishment.

She went across the room and returned with her bullwhip. She pulled down the panties which she herself had put on him.

"Take that, you little bitch!" she shouted as she began whipping his buttocks with all her might. Slash after slash tore right through the skin on both sides of his ass.

"Mommy! Mommy!" he exclaimed and then let out a noise that sounded like a combination of crying and moaning.

She then took out a canister of salt and rubbed both of her hands in it, and proceeded to spank his ass while rubbing salt into the wounds caused by the whipping. His screams were terrible. He begged and pleaded for her to stop, but it only seemed to strengthen her resolve and fuel her anger.

"You fucking, FUCKING little whore!" she screamed and started shoving her fingers into his asshole. First two and then three fingers, and then four, she continued to dilate his ass until she had almost half of her hand in his rectum.

"I have known cum sucking little whores like you my whole life!" she said and with a lurch forward and pushing with her legs too, she shoved her entire fist into his butt.

"Aaahh! Aaah! Aahhh!" was all that Lechoslaw could say. He felt his heart racing, and a strange feeling running through the lower part of his body. He was panting increasingly harder and his head was swimming. "AAAAAAhhhhhhh!" he screamed as he ejaculated! He had just had the first orgasm of his life, and no one was even touching his penis.

Chapter 2: Camp

Love at First Sight

"Fuck!" thought Bozydar "summer camp - I hate it!" After looking forward to the summer throughout the school year, Bozydar's father informed him that he had no choice but to go to camp, while the rest of the family went on vacation.

After getting off the bus with his backpack and getting a room assigned to him, Bozydar headed over to the main assembly hall, which also served as the cafeteria; all the boys had been called together for the first camp meeting. He was sure that he would hate the meeting, because the camp counselors were surely fucking assholes and idiots!

He filed in surrounded by the other campers, most of who were excited and joking with each other and generally having a good time.

As the head counselor began to address the happy campers, Bozydar's mind drifted off. He wasn't listening anyway, and he stared off into the crowd of boys, thinking about what idiots they all were.

Then it happened, one boy's face grabbed his attention. He wasn't sure why, but he felt incredibly attracted to this boy. He felt as though he had never seen anyone so good looking before. This boy was almost pretty. He also missed his dog, which he eventually named "Lucky" before it decomposed into nothing but a pile of bones.

Then Bozydar noticed that the boy was also staring back at him. He saw this lovely face smile at him, and he smiled back.

Lechoslaw had looked forward to camp very much. It was time away from his mother, and he loved being with other boys. He got a crush on a different boy every year at camp, but had never met someone who was openly gay, so he kept it to himself.

As Lechoslaw stared around at the other boys in the first camp meeting, his eyes met with a boy who was the most radiant gorgeous thing he had ever seen. He fell in love immediately, and smiled at the boy who was staring at him. The boy smiled back, and he hoped for a summer camp love tryst.

He decided to introduce himself to the boy as soon as the meeting was over, and waited impatiently as the head counselor continued to address the assembled campers.

BFFs

The head counselor went through a dissertation about all of the activities they had planned for the campers, and introduced the rest of the staff and counselors. He also explained the schedule, and told them that Lights Out is at Twenty One Hundred hours.

Finally, the meeting was concluded, and they boys were told that they could have fun until dinner. When they heard the camp bell ringing, they were to return to the cafeteria for their evening meal.

As soon as the room started to clear, Bozydar and Lechoslaw quickly made their way across the crowded room towards each other.

"Hi. I am Bozydar."

"It's nice to meet you. I'm Lechoslaw."

"It's very nice to meet you Lechoslaw!" said Bozydar as he extended his hand for a handshake.

The boys shook hands while staring into each other's eyes, and continued to hold hands long after the handshake had ended.

"Do you like hiking Lechoslaw?" asked Bozydar.

"Oh yes! I *love* hiking!" was the response, and the boys headed over to one of the many trails surrounding the camp. There were many campers who went for a hike after the meeting, so the boys chose a path that looked obscure and secluded.

After hiking a short way up the trail, Bozydar reached over gently and slid his hand into Lechoslaw's hand, which was receptive to the gesture. Again, the boys looked into each other's eyes as they walked.

Lechoslaw: "God you are hansom!"

"I am glad that you think so! I think that you are pretty. Do you want to be my girlfriend?" responded Bozydar.

"There is *nothing* that I would like more!" replied Lechoslaw.

"Is there some place that we can sit down?" asked Bozydar.

Lechoslaw went to this camp every year, and knew the trails well. He guided Bozydar up the path to a secluded grove where a large log provided a nice bench to sit on.

The boys sat down next to each other, and Bozydar slid both an arm and a leg around Lechoslaw.

Bozydar leaned in and kissed Lechoslaw slowly on the lips. He then kissed his nose, his left cheek, and then his right cheek in that order. "I want to be best friends forever." He said. "Me too" Lechoslaw said with a sigh.

Bozydar returned to Lechoslaw's lips, and gently pried them apart with his tongue. He slid his tongue between his lover's lips, and found the quarry he sought, his sweet velvety tongue.

As tongues slid together Bozydar began massaging Lechoslaw's chest as though he were making out with a girl. Lechoslaw could feel his heart beating faster, and slid his right hand up Bozydar's thigh and squeezed his crotch, which was hot and he could feel it swelling in his hand.

"Go ahead." said Bozydar softly "Take it out."

With that, Lechoslaw kneeled between Bozydar's legs and opened his fly. The largest and most beautiful penis he had ever seen emerged from Bozydar's briefs, fully erect and throbbing.

Lechoslaw placed his mouth over Bozydar's stiff cock and started moving his head up and down.

"God that feels good, but I don't want to cum in your mouth. Let me put it in your butt."

Lechoslaw loved the feeling of the hot stiff rod in his mouth, but he wanted to make Bozydar happy, and he thought that it probably would not hurt nearly as much as the things his mother did to him.

"Okay, but it is a little sore." said Lechoslaw, "My mother has a really *unusual* way of taking my temperature."

Lechoslaw removed his pants and pulled down his underwear, then leaned over the log with his posterior exposed.

"My God you have a beautiful ass!" exclaimed Bozydar, who was smearing some saliva on the end of his cock.

"Give it to me baby!" said Lechoslaw, who was yearning to feel his lover's dick in his ass.

Bozydar began to push the head of his dick into Lechoslaw's wanting anus.

Suddenly, they were both shocked by a loud noise. Someone was shouting!

Caught in the Act

"JUST WHAT IN THE FUCKING HELL DO YOU THINK YOU'RE DOING?" screamed the counselor, who had apparently followed them up the trail.

"We... uh..." stammered Lechoslaw.

"Save it!" snapped the counselor.

The counselor was a tall muscular man, and very angry too. He grabbed one arm on each boy and walked them straight back to camp and to the main office where the head counselor was tending some minor business.

"What's all this?" asked the head counselor.

"You wouldn't believe it! I caught these boys butt-fucking!"

"Well," said the head counselor, "We can't have that! You boys really *have* been bad! So you like to take it in the butt do you?"

Both boys just looked at each other, then back down at the floor.

"Answer me!" he demanded "Do you like to take it in the butt?"

"No." said Bozydar, "*I* do not like to take it in the butt. *He* likes to take it in the butt. I like to *give* it in the butt!"

"You little bastard! How dare you get sarcastic with me! It's the paddle for you for sure! In the mean time, you two will be put in isolation while we decide what your punishment will be."

With that, Bozydar and Lechoslaw are lead to different rooms and locked in.

Cornholed

Back at the main camp office, the counselors discussed what punishment would be appropriate for their crime.

"Well I can paddle them both" said the head counselor, "but I am not sure that we can punish them hard enough to discourage them from behaving this way in the future."

The man who caught them in the act then spoke up. "I have an idea that I am really excited about. Look at it this way, we are at *camp* right? What could be a better way to convince someone that he does *not* like a thing than to give him *too much of it?*"

Satisfied, he went back to the office to look up the phone numbers of the boys' parents.

Lechoslaw was enjoying his punishment. He mused to himself that it was not nearly as painful as his mother's punishments. If the camp administrators tell his mother about what he was caught doing, there will be hell to pay!

The boys' punishment went on day after day after day. They were not fed, nor allowed to go to a bathroom to relieve themselves. To Bozydar and Lechoslaw, it was just like an endless sea of cocks, one right after another all day and all night. The head counselor was unable to get Bozydar's parents on the telephone, because they were on vacation.

Lechoslaw's mother was drunk and didn't give a damn, but she had also gotten her phone service cut off due to non-payment of her bill.

A week after their punishment had started Bozydar's family finally returned from their vacation and went to pick him up at the camp. They are greeted by the camp head counselor.

"You must be Bozydar's dad. You won't believe what we caught him doing! He was getting frisky with another one of the campers! I mean, *sexually*, you know?" he said.

"What? He was trying to fuck a little girl?" said Bozydar's father, outraged.

"No." said the head counselor, "He was trying to fuck a *boy*."

The head counselor said that they had already punished Bozydar, and that he probably wouldn't try it again, but that he recommended additional disciplinary action at home. Bozydar's father agreed and assured the head counselor that he would be punished **severely** upon returning home.

When the drunken mess that was Lechoslaw's mother finally showed up five days later, the head counselor told her what her boy had done. There was fire in her eyes!

Punishment

When she got Lechoslaw home, he was starving, but she sent him straight to the basement and locked him in, then proceeded to get herself a strong drink. She drank it quickly and made herself another drink, even stronger this time. This went on for at least an hour, until she was totally obliterated. By the time she showed up in the basement with a cantaloupe and a jar of lubricant she couldn't even remember why she was punishing him!

Bozydar's father, on the other hand, was only too aware of what his boy had done to warrant punishment. He had beaten Bozydar nearly to death on several occasions, but it had never prevented further misbehavior on his part. He now wanted to punish him more than ever, but he wanted his son to be humiliated too.

He went to his woodshop and picked up a large claw hammer, and then went to Bozydar's bedroom, where he had been grounded.

Handing the hammer to Bozydar, he said "Take it."

"No, Dad, please!" the boy pleaded.

"If you don't take the hammer, I will hit you with it myself! DO YOU WANT THAT?" His father was in a rage.

Bozydar was terrified, and took the hammer from his father with a trembling hand.

"Now hit yourself with it." His father said.

Bozydar knew that he had no choice. He was furious with his father and in his own mind thought about hitting his father with the hammer each time he struck himself in the head. The pain was unbearable.

Ostracized

Bozydar was left to suffer for hours. He was later called downstairs. When he entered the dining room, his entire family was there including some cousins, aunts, and uncles.

His father spoke: "I called you all here to deal with the sad news that we found out that our son Bozydar is a homosexual."

Celestynka: "Yea... Right..." She said, rolling her eyes upwardly in sarcasm.

He then turned to Bozydar's Grandmother. "Mother, you are the matriarch of this family. We will decide upon Bozydar's punishment based on your council."

Grandmother: "There is only one way to deal with this kind of shame. We must ostracize Bozydar."

She then stood and pointed at Bozydar and shouted, "Bozydar, you are no longer a member of this family! You are dead to me! No one here is to speak your name ever again! You don't exist to any of us! Furthermore, you will never be going back to that camp, so you will also never see your little girlfriend ever again!"

Bozydar was allowed to live in his room, but no one in the family ever spoke to him after he had been ostracized.

Chapter 3:
The Nazis are Cumming

Ten years passed, and Bozydar and Lechoslaw had grown tall and strong. Bozydar was an enormous brute with huge muscles and towering at six and a half feet in height. Lechoslaw was much shorter, and maintained an effeminate demeanor and appearance.

It is now 1939, and many Jewish families are becoming nervous because of the political situation in Poland.

Bozydar's father called together and addresses his household.

"Our world is becoming more dangerous. I saw three more Jewish families on this street taken into custody today." He said.

"The Heisensteins were taken yesterday, and the Nazis shot poor old mister Goldman in the head just for being Jewish!" added his wife.

"Honey", he continued, turning to Celestynka, "I don't want you to go to school tomorrow."

Celestynka: "Okay Daddy."

The following day, Bozydar was retuning home and as he approached his house, he saw military vehicles and trucks in the street, and men adorned with swastikas and armed with rifles approaching the front door of his home. He rushed forward as a soldier kicked it in. The soldiers enter his home and he ran up shouting, "No! No!"

The first soldier he approached knocked him out with the butt of his gun. When he came to, he and his father were both in shackles, and he saw three Nazi soldiers gang-raping his mother, one in each of her holes. There were also two Nazis fucking Celestynka in the mouth, while another was fucking her vagina, and two more in her asshole. The rape continued until all of the soldiers and officers in the company were completely satisfied. Celestynka nearly drown in all of the cum being squirted into her mouth and all over her face. She was only fifteen years of age, and as far as Bozydar knew, she was still a virgin, before this day.

The entire family was then bound and led out of the house. They were assembled with at least twenty other Jewish families in the neighborhood.

A high ranking Nazi officer addressed his men: "Have all of these Jews been sodomized?" The answer came back as "No."

"Okay", he went on, "I want all of you Jews to form two lines. Everyone who has already been sodomized form an orderly line to get onto these trucks. Any of you who have *not* been sodomized yet, form a line right here to get sodomized prior to boarding the vehicles. Do you understand?"

Most of the Jews complied grudgingly, but Bozydar got into the line of those who have already been sodomized. "I have had enough of that!" He thought to himself, and allowed himself to be herded onto one of the trucks.

When the Nazis came, Lechoslaw was not so lucky. He had come home, and his mother was totally drunk as usual. She even passed out before she could confine him to the basement for his nightly punishment with no dinner.

He was just counting himself lucky when the Nazis kicked in the front door.

He was made to watch as they gang raped his semi-conscious mother. They went out of their way to penetrate every one of her orifices with as many cocks as they could simultaneously. Lechoslaw was impressed, because they were *pretty good* at it!

Lechoslaw didn't feel sorry for her. Fuck her! If anyone deserves it, that person is *her*! He even envied her, and wished that he was the center of that attention. He was sure that he could take that many cocks at once and survive.

By the time the Nazis were finished, Lechoslaw's mother was no longer moving. In fact, she wasn't breathing either. One of the Nazi's kicked her in the ribs and exclaimed, "Fucking Jew! You fucking disgust me!"

Auschwitz

The group of prisoners that Bozydar was in had been transferred to a train during the night, and it was now pulling into Auschwitz.

Looking out, he could see a detention area in which families were being split up, and people were being put in lines and sorted out.

The old, the children, the sick, the injured, and the handicapped were all being stripped bare and sent to take a shower.

The biggest and strongest young men were being placed in a separate holding area.

More disturbingly, bodily cavity searches were being performed on nearly every prisoner, and the Nazis were gangbanging many of the children after stripping them naked.

As Bozydar was shoved out of the train by a very rough guard, he saw a Nazi officer point to him and tell a couple of guards, "That one - take that big strong one there!"

The two guards then escorted Bozydar to the holding pen with several other men who all looked like they could carry a load. Perhaps they feared strong Jews the most, and were planning on killing them first because they appear most able to fight. Bozydar feared the worst.

Incinerator

Lechoslaw was practically in shock by the time he was pulled from the train and severely beaten by several guards. It was not clear to him why they were doing it.

He was then lead to a building with four large smoke stacks billowing dark smoke.

He was forced to walk down a ramp and entered through a basement door. Inside, he saw piles of dead bodies and four large incinerators, with doors big enough to fit a human body into them.

One of the guards hit Lechoslaw with the butt of his rifle, and forced him over to the closest incinerator.

"Well, I guess this is It." thought Lechoslaw.

He wondered what it will be like to burn alive in that thing. I knew that he would enjoy the pain, and it would probably make him come in his pants. At the same time, he was afraid to die.

With some hesitation, Lechoslaw walked over to the mouth of the chamber and opened the door, and began to climb in.

The guard who had struck Lechoslaw shoved him to the floor.

"No!" said the guard, "You fucking idiot Jew! These chambers are for the disposal of dead bodies. Do you understand? See that pile of corpses on that cart? Your job is to feed them into these chambers."

"Go get one and put it in." He went on. "Lock the door after it has been loaded, then turn this lever and press the red button."

"When the incineration is complete, pull this handle and the ashes will fall into the catch pan below, which you will empty once a day. If you do your job, you will be fed, if you don't, then I *will* put you in one of these myself!"

Lechoslaw thought about what a grizzly job he had to do, but he now heaved a sigh of relief, and figured that he was one of the lucky ones.

Doom

Bozydar is taken from the holding pen along with four other men. As they were marched across the compound, each of the men was dropped off at a different building. He also noticed corpses being removed from several of the buildings. He knew that this is where the Nazis did their killing.

"They are leading me to my doom!" Bozydar thought to himself. "Fuck it! I have had a fucking miserable life anyway!"

The Nazi guards lead Bozydar up to the front door of one of the buildings. The one in front opened the door.

Chapter 4: The Gas Chamber

The door opened, and Bozydar could see dead corpses stripped bare piled everywhere in the room. He had thought that he was being taken to an empty chamber to die, and suddenly realized that they wanted something else.

"What's your name?" asked one guard.

"Bozydar"

"Okay, Bozydar, you are being given a job. Pick up all of the dead bodies in this room and put them in these hand carts. When you are done, I will show you where to take them. When this chamber is cleared, we want you to start on the one next door. Is that clear?"

He saw naked children being lead into the building next to the one he was standing in front of.

"Yes." He replied.

Bozydar realized that the guards didn't want to touch a bunch of dirty dead naked Jews. Many of them had evacuated themselves when they died, so the smell was awful and the mess was beyond description!

Bozydar began picking up bodies and placing them in the cart. It was actually pretty easy work, but they were freshly dead, and rigor mortis had not set in, so they were all limp deadweight. Some of the people were from his community, and occasionally he would recognize a face.

When Bozydar finished clearing out the entire room, he was lead to an identical building right next to the one where he had been working. When the guards opened the door, it also was filled with dead bodies, but this time they were all children and babies. Not one of them looked like it was over fifteen years of age.

He started to clear the chamber out, and found that he could carry several babies and children at the same time, because they were so tiny. Clearing the room went far more quickly than the previous chamber, which had contained mostly old people.

He saw a skinny blond girl lying on her stomach and he thought about how nice a butt she had. He rolled her over and was shocked to recognize the pale face of Celestynka!

"Those fucking Nazi bastards!" he thought, and started to cry as he pulled her close in his arms and started to kiss her face. He kissed the lips that he wanted so much in life. He mourned and realized that he had always been in love with her, now he would never have her as his wife.

In spite of his sadness, he suddenly realized that he was getting an erection. "Why not?" he thought. "After all no one is in here but me. The guards don't appear to come in."

He pulled out his cock and began to penetrate her vagina. She had recently died, so she was still a bit warm, and he kissed her as he made passionate love to her. He suddenly realized that he was finally doing something that he had longed for most of his life.

"You can't get away from me know, can you?" he said to Celestynka. After a raging orgasm in her pussy, Bozydar rolled his sister over and stuffed his cock into her asshole. He craned her head back and put his tongue into her mouth as he cornholed her in the ass the way he had always wanted to.

He knew that the guards would be displeased if he didn't finish quickly, but he was already ahead on this job anyway.

He decided to sodomize his sister in the mouth as a way of saying goodbye to her.

Chapter 5:
Making the Best of It

Knowing that Celestynka was dead made Bozydar realize how precarious his position was. He was only allowed to live as long as the guards allow him to. Having their good favor was more important than the worth of the diamond ring.

He went up to the guards who stood outside the gas chamber.

Guard: "What do you want? Have you finished?"

Bozydar: "Yes, I am done. Here. I found this inside one of the bodies. You can have it." Bozydar handed the ring over to the guard.

Guard: "You are a fast worker. You are honest too? Excellent! From now on, you are to consider double checking every mouth, vagina, and asshole part of your job. We have more work for you. Push that cart you filled and follow me."

The guards escorted him over to the incinerator building.

Guard: "Leave the cart at the top of the ramp and someone will bring it inside. Every time you fill a cart, leave it right here. If they start to pile up, then help bring the carts down the ramp and inside. The first chamber you cleared out is full again. Clear it out now while we fill the other one."

Bozydar went back to work. Since all the bodies were naked, it was a simple matter to rape them. It was now his job to do bodily cavity searches, so he just kept his dick out and shoved it into every hole in every corpse. He ended up finding a lot more jewelry and money, and one corpse had a potato shoved up her snatch. He handed it all over to the guards, who praised him as their best chamber clearer ever.

Every time he opened the door of a newly filled chamber, he looked in at a sea of naked bodies, and he knew that he would be fucking every one of them. He felt a marvelous sense of job satisfaction, and a feeling of contentment came over him as he had never before experienced.

Grandmother

Bozydar was whistling while he worked. He loved his job, and couldn't remember ever doing anything in his life that he enjoyed so much.

He removed his dick from an old woman's asshole and rolled her over. He was suddenly surprised when he saw the face of his dead grandmother! He shoved his cock in her dusty old vagina (which was actually still warm, as she had only been dead for a few minutes) and became enraged as he thought back to being ostracized by her. He had lost his whole family for life because of this nasty, mean old crone! He raged as his mind is filled with hatred and anger towards her!

"You old fucking cunt bitch!" He screamed as he thought about how she always had hated him.

Bozydar then looked down and saw both of his fists covered in blood. He realized that he had smashed her face in completely as he was raping her dead corpse.

The thought then came to him that his vengeance against her was complete, and for the first time in his life, he felt a sense of victory.

Father

The next day, Bozydar was only half way through clearing one of his chambers when he found himself staring at his father's face.

"My God!" he exclaimed, "This is too good to be true!"

Bozydar had always hated his father, and the feeling was mutual. His father had always adored Celestynka, and treated Bozydar like shit!

Bozydar angrily anally raped his father's dead corpse with enthusiasm! He pulled his cock out of its anus and then kicked the corpse over and over. He punched his father in the face and thought back to the time when he had fractured his arm and two ribs, and given him a concussion with a wrench.

"Who's doing the beating *now* you old pile of crap!" he shouted as he pulverized what remained of his father's corpse. He continued to shout obscenely as he shit and pissed on the corpse.

When he was done, there was virtually nothing left of his father's head, so he fucked the stump of his next. He decided to call this procedure a "pulp fuck."

A great feeling of satisfaction and victory came over Bozydar. "Two enemies in two days - nice!" he thought to himself.

It's A Dirty Job

Every morning, Lechoslaw would look
forward to his day's work. The guards were
cruel to him, and he enjoyed their beatings.

As he fed bodies into incinerators,
Lechoslaw whistled a lively tune and
thought about how the dead are the lucky
ones. A deep feeling of job satisfaction came
over him as well.

He wondered what it would be like to be
burned alive in one of those incinerators.
The pain would be excruciating. "I wonder
if I would enjoy it." he thought to himself.

Lechoslaw felt his penis becoming erect
thinking about horrible amounts of pain. In
the evening before falling asleep, he
regularly masturbated as he imagined the
excruciating agony of being burned alive.

"You fucking cumsucking dirty pile of shit Jew!" The guard shouted as he kicked Lechoslaw over and over again.

A second guard joined in and kicked Lechoslaw in the stomach. Yet another guard drew his baton and struck him in the head.

Lechoslaw was getting his ass kicked by the guards again, which seemed to happen on a regular basis.

Even though he was entirely capable of keeping up with the pace of the flow of dead corpses he was to incinerate, he would lag behind intentionally, because he knew that it infuriated the guards, who would in turn get chewed out if the quota was not kept up.

The guards continued to kick Lechoslaw and beat him with their weapons until they were exhausted.

When the beating is over, Lechoslaw felt a familiar wetness in his underwear. There was a warm feeling in the back too.

Pretty Girl

and noticed something in her nose. Once he had finished eating her cunt, he pulled from her nose what turned out to be a large booger, and decided to have it for desert.

Bully

Later on that day, he was clearing a chamber when he recognized a man his own age who he recognized as the bully who had beaten him up in the schoolyard years before. "I am going to do a special on you!" he thought to himself. He kicked the crap out of the bully's corpse and sodomized it orally and anally.

Bozydar thought about all of the enemies who he had hated when he was younger, who he had since fucked in their warm freshly dead and still pliable assholes!

In spite of fucking assholes all day or perhaps because of it, every evening before falling asleep, Bozydar would masturbate and think about all the people who had been killed that day. He had come to feel that what they were doing was a form of art. He comes while thinking about how he gets to fuck almost every Jew he sees.

Chapter 7: Reunited

Bozydar pulled his cock out of an asshole, and loaded the final corpse on his hand cart, which was now full to overflowing. He lifted the handles, and started to push it towards the incinerator building.

As he approached the ramp, he could see a man lying on the ground who was being beaten viciously by the guards. Bozydar had always loved hurting people, and secretly wanted to join in the fun.

Bozydar wheeled up the cartload of fresh dead bodies.

"Hey, you there! Come over here and help him catch up!" shouted one of the guards.

The guards then forced Bozydar to assist the prisoner who was still on the ground.

When he helped the man to his feet, he could not believe his eyes!

Lechoslaw was in agony after the guards' beating. A strong Jewish man took his arm and helped him to his feet. When he looked up he saw before him the boy whom he fell so in love with at camp ten years before! Bozydar smiled back at him and put his finger over his mouth. "Sssshhh." The lovers were ecstatic to be reunited, but were careful to not let the guards know.

The next day, Lechoslaw made certain that he did not fall behind on incinerations. In fact, he was ahead if anything. He couldn't wait for Bozydar to show up with another load of bodies. He had never fallen out of love with Bozydar, and had feared that he would never see him again. The anticipation was killing him, so he filled up all four incinerators, and fired them up!

When Bozydar delivered a load of corpses that morning, he pushed the cart right down the ramp and brought it inside.

When Lechoslaw saw Bozydar enter with another load of dead bodies, he rushed to his lover's arms.

Bozydar threw Lechoslaw onto the pile of corpses and tore his pants off. He then stuck his tongue in his lover anus. He used his tongue to lubricate and stretch Lechoslaw's asshole and then shoved in his throbbing penis.

He rammed all nine inches of his cock up Lechoslaw's asshole and felt his balls rubbing on his lover's ass cheeks. "I missed you so much!" he exclaimed.

Bozydar: "Do you remember that this is what we were doing when we got caught?"

Lechoslaw nodded, but only moaned. His face was pressed into dead people, and he could see that several of them had been gnawed on.

Bozydar continued to ram his cock in and out of Lechoslaw's soft anus until he achieved a raging orgasm.

When he pulled his cock out of Lechoslaw, it had a large lump of smelly brown shit on it. "Shit." He said.

Lechoslaw: "Is that my ice cream cone?"

Bozydar smiled. "Yes little girl, you may eat it now..."

Lechoslaw leaped off of the pile of corpses upon which he had just been cornholed, and dropped enthusiastically to his knees. He shoved Bozydar's entire cock down his throat, turd and all. He pulled the cock back out of his throat and began to nibble and lick at the edges of the turd ball which was still attached to the head of his lover's dick. He continued to lick the shit covered cock as though he were eating a lolly pop. He nibbled away slowly at the shit until he had devoured it completely, and then started to suck on Bozydar's mighty dong.

Bozydar came a second time, and blew his load entirely into Lechoslaw's mouth.

Lechoslaw swallowed all of the shit, and all of the cum too.

"God it feels good to fuck the living." said Bozydar. "I have never fucked someone who is alive before."

Lechoslaw: "I have never been fucked by anyone but my mother."

The lovers kissed then got back to work before the guards could catch them. Bozydar helped Lechoslaw incinerate bodies, and the two men working together got the job done over twice as fast as it would normally take.

Bozydar French kissed Lechoslaw and fondled his ass and said, "Now you save that sweet ass for me, my love." With that he picked up the handles of the now empty hand truck and pushed it back up the ramp and back to the gas chambers.

Bozydar fell asleep that evening feeling happier than he had ever been. He had a job that he loved and was appreciated for. He had a lover who would never have been accepted in the culture that he was from, and he got to have a final vengeance over almost every enemy he has ever had. On top of all that, he was in necrophiliac heaven!

Lechoslaw fell asleep that night praying to God and thanking him for giving him the opportunity to be with the love of his life. He thanked God for everything that He had done for the Jewish people, and for Auschwitz and for the Holocaust, without which he and his lover would not be together.

Chapter 8:
Something Borrowed

The Experiment

Nazi Officer: "Doctor Strumfatha, you have the floor."

Doctor: "Officers and gentlemen, thank you. Our facility has a number of interesting projects going on at this time. One project that I think you will find interesting addresses my hypothesis that Jews are not really people, and therefore it is morally correct to continue to exterminate them."

"I have conceived a series of experiments in which we ask Jews to perform the most horrible and monstrous acts we can think up, and see how much encouragement it takes to get them to do it."

"Today's experiment involves two average Jewish workers who we have borrowed from a nearby concentration camp. We won't tell them what the experiment's true purpose is, but we will ask them to pour molten silver down the throat of an infant. Data collection will be focused on their reaction to the situation."

Borrowed

Lechoslaw was just finishing up incinerating a load of corpses when an important looking Nazi officer who he had never seen before entered with four very grim guards.

"You! Come with us! Hurry!" said the officer.

The second he stepped through the door, a hood was thrown over his head, and he felt the wind knocked out of him as a rifle butt was rammed into his solar plexus. He fell to the ground, and the guards shackled him and dragged him over to a truck.

He was thrown into the back of the truck and found himself with other prisoners. He could hear people breathing and chains moving, but there was little talking. They probably thought that whatever was going to happen to them would not be good.

"Bozydar?" said Lechoslaw.

"Yes, I am right here." replied Bozydar.

Well, at least they would be together, whatever was to happen.

Bozydar and Lechoslaw were driven to a nearby medical facility, which was being used as a Nazi research center, mostly focused on torturing Jews for various sadistic reasons.

When they arrived, they were brought inside by guards, where the doctor was waiting.

"You are probably wondering why you have been brought here." said the doctor, "We are studying the subject of how much pain a Jew can take. You two have been selected to help us with an experiment. You should consider this an honor."

Lechoslaw became excited at the thought of being tortured. "Mmmmmmm…." he thought to himself and imagined being torn apart slowly.

Bozydar's face lit up. "You mean we get to torture people?" asked Bozydar.

"Yes", the doctor replied.

Bozydar thought about what a fun time this was going to be! He felt a pounding in his heart and a swelling in his genitals.

Bozydar and Lechoslaw are taken to a room with smelting equipment and a small forge. They see a pot of molten silver sitting in the forge. They look at each other and know that someone is going to get hurt. They are told to wait and after a while they heard screaming down the hall.

The door then opened, and a nurse brought in a naked infant girl, about 18 months old. From back down the hall, they could hear a woman screaming.

"My baby! Please bring her back!" was the cry.

The infant was also screaming and howling as she was placed on the work bench.

The doctor then came in and explained the procedure.

Doctor: "This experiment has to do with physical pain. Our data collection will be based on the level of pain experienced by this infant. Do you understand?"

Both lovers told the doctor that they understand the nature of the experiment.

Doctor: "You two are to pour molten silver down the baby's throat. I suggest that one of you should hold the infant steady while the other pours the silver."

Bozydar: "I am the stronger. I should hold it."

They were taken back to the truck, and
Lechoslaw was beaten again for no
particular reason before they were returned
to their normal duties.

Chapter 9: Bliss

Kudos

Commandant Hoss called his top officers together for a meeting.

Hoss: "Hitler is very pleased. Our efficiency in processing Jews is higher than it has ever been, and he has commissioned several new facilities based on the methods that we have developed here in Auschwitz. Also we are all to receive promotions."

The assembly applauded enthusiastically.

He went on, "Apparently, we have some of the most contented and hard working prisoners anywhere in the Empire. This speaks well of the performance of you and your men. Our productivity is up and Hitler and I have never been happier. I personally am recommending each of you for a commendation to accompany your promotion."

The officers applaud even louder.

Hoss concluded with the following comments, "Even our working prisoners are appreciated. It is their good attitude and hard work that has allowed us to become so efficient and productive. It is through the efforts of a few hard working Jews that we have been able to become so effective at exterminating their people."

Utopia

After a hard day's work, Lechoslaw and Bozydar snuck back to Bozydar's bunk. Bozydar slid his arms gently around his lover and proceeded to kiss his head and face softly.

Lechoslaw: "I am happier than I have ever been Bozydar."

Bozydar: "Me too, my love."

Lechoslaw: "My life has always been pain. Everyone I have ever met has hurt me, except for you."

Bozydar: "I feel the same way. You are the only living person I have ever made love with."

Lechoslaw: "My mother would never have allowed me to be with you. She would never have allowed me to love anyone."

Bozydar: "My parents swore that we would never be together again. Now they are all dead, and I personally fucked every one of them! And I have you in my arms. This is the sweetest feeling I have ever had."

Lechoslaw: "I have had crushes, but I have never loved anyone else. I was glad when I watched that vicious whore gang raped to death."

Bozydar: "I am happy for you."

Lechoslaw: "Bozydar? I noticed that the last load of corpses you brought were all missing their genitalia."

Bozydar: "Well… I see no reason to waste the meat. They serve us so little food here. I have taken to eating the genitals off of every corpse that I fuck."

Lechoslaw smiles and says, "I guess you can also be thankful for being well fed too. Were it not for the Nazis, we might never have found each other again. I give thanks every night to God for you, and for our togetherness."

Bozydar: "Me too. I cannot even count all my blessings. I have a great job, and they love my work! I am truly in love for the first time, and I *love* making love with you. I am appreciated, and better at what I do than anyone. I have sex with hundreds of people every day, and I eat the best cuisine!"

Lechoslaw: "We are both happier than we ever have been, and probably than we ever could have been in the world in which we grew up. Our love would *never* have been accepted by our families. I give praise and thanks to God for Hitler's genius, for the Nazis, for the Holocaust, and especially for Auschwitz!"

The lovers made love and then Lechoslaw drifted off and fell asleep in Bozydar's arms.

Chapter 10: It Couldn't Last

It is 1943, and Rudolf Hoss hosted Arthur Liebehenschel on a tour of the Auschwitz facility, in preparation for handing over his command.

Liebehenschel: "I was very impressed by the incinerators. I would like very much to get a closer look at the gas chambers, and how they are run."

Hoss: "Of course Her Liebehenschel. I am so glad that you are enjoying yourself." He smiles. "We are very enthusiastic about our work here. The gas chambers are next on your tour. I will bring you to our most efficient units."

The Nazi officers continued to chat as they strolled from the incinerator building towards the gas chambers followed by an entourage of assistants and guards.

Hoss knew that the chambers that ran the most efficiently were the ones attended by Bozydar, who loved his work passionately, so they were the ones he would show off to Liebehenschel.

When they reached the gas chamber that Bozydar was in the process of clearing, Hoss

and without hesitation, Hoss removed his sidearm from its holster and discharged it into Bozydar's skull at point blank range.

Bozydar's lifeless corpse fell to the floor.

"Get another chamber clearing team over here and clean up this chamber, starting with *that*." said Hoss, pointing at Bozydar's dead body.

Chapter 11: Oblivion Together

Lechoslaw hummed a tune as he worked, and had a contented smile on his face. He looked forward to the end of the day, when he would once again feel his lover's large hot penis inside his body.

He emptied a cart one corpse at a time, and thought about how happy and how deeply in love he was.

At the bottom of the cart, Lechoslaw discovered something unusual. A corpse, face down, with clothing still on. A large majority of the corpses delivered on the carts are naked, so he thought this odd.

Further, the corpse was dressed in the standard uniform for Jewish workers in Auschwitz.

Lechoslaw noticed that the color of the hair and the sheer size of the corpse was the same as Bozydar. A cold dagger sliced into Lechoslaw's heart and he rolled the corpse over.

Lechoslaw let out a blood curdling scream as he stared down upon his dead lover. He cradled Bozydar in his arm and lamented aloud. He kissed him and began to undress his dead lover's corpse.

Lechoslaw removed Bozydar's pants and shorts, and leaned over him crying and swirled his flaccid cock around in his mouth.

Two guards had heard the scream and entered the room to see what the source of the screaming was.

They walked in and saw the incinerator attendant performing fellatio on the corpse of another dead Jew.

The guards ran over to Lechoslaw. "Get that out of your mouth you dirty fucking Jew!" one of them shouted, as the other struck Lechoslaw in the head with the butt of his rifle.

The two guards shouted obscenities at Lechoslaw and beat him within and inch of his life with their weapons.

"You vile piece of shit! We will no longer put up with you!" one of the guards said.

The guards then made Lechoslaw strip himself naked, and gave him a final beating.

They put Bozydar's body into an incinerator.

"You get to join him, you dirty fucking Jewish faggot!" snapped one of the guards.

The guards grabbed Lechoslaw by his arms and forced him into the incinerator with his lover's dead body.

Lechoslaw always had wondered what it would be like to burn to death, but he was afraid to die anyway. When the incinerator door was slammed shut and latched, he knew that there was no way out. He grabbed one of Bozydar's hands and shoved it as far up his ass as it would go. He heard the familiar hiss of the gas being turned on. He went down and shoved Bozydar's cock into his mouth.

The Nazi guard hit the red button that ignited the burners.

As the flames began to deliver the searing agony which Lechoslaw so loved, he had the best orgasm of his life while sucking Bozydar's dead cock, and thought, "At least it's oblivion together, my love!"